A MOST EXTRAORDINARY CAT

Jim chewed his lower lip. The animal facing him suddenly yawned, showing needle-pointed teeth and a curling, rough-coated tongue. It was the largest and blackest cat Jim had ever seen. In the sun its fur gleamed as if each shining hair had a tiny rainbow tip. Between its green eyes there sprouted an odd, thin V-shape of white hairs, and the very tips of its four paws were also white.

The cat stared compellingly at Jim. Jim did not know very much about cats, but he did know that this was no scrawny stray. . . . This cat was not afraid of him in the least. . . . Did all cats just sit and watch you this way? As if they could see into your head and know what you were thinking?

About the Authors and Illustrator:

ANDRE NORTON has written more than seventy books, which have been published both in the United States and abroad, and have appeared in several languages. She has received numerous writing and science fiction awards. Formerly a children's librarian, she now devotes her full time to her writing.

DOROTHY MADLEE works as a staff news feature writer for the Orlando, Florida *Sentinel Star,* and has received awards and citations for her news stories. Her adult short stories and science fiction pieces have appeared in national magazines.

BERNARD COLONNA designed and illustrated several major promotional pieces for the International Paper Company, and has illustrated a number of children's books.

STAR KA'AT

ANDRE NORTON
and
DOROTHY MADLEE

illustrated by
BERNARD COLONNA

AN ARCHWAY PAPERBACK
POCKET BOOKS · NEW YORK

STAR KA'AT

Walker edition published 1976

Archway Paperback edition published August, 1977

Published by
POCKET BOOKS, a Simon & Schuster Division of
GULF & WESTERN CORPORATION
1230 Avenue of the Americas, New York, N.Y. 10020.

Archway Paperback editions are distributed in the U.S. by
Simon & Schuster, Inc., 1230 Avenue of the Americas,
New York, N.Y. 10020, and in Canada by Simon & Schuster
of Canada, Ltd., Markham, Ontario, Canada.

1287

For Impy,
Surely a Star Ka'at

CONTENTS

1 TWO AND TWO 1

2 TIRO, MER AND PROBLEMS 19

3 THE SHADOW HANGS DARK 35

4 THE LAST ORDER 51

5 "GOING TO FIND US
A HOME PLACE—" 69

6 JIM AND ELLY IN SEARCH 85

7 KA'AT JUSTICE 101

1

Two and Two

THE MUGGY, hot summer weather had settled on Washington. Carefully, Jim Evans crept under the loose board in the fence. Beyond was a tangle of weeds high enough to hide him if he kept on his knees as he worked his way to where the wrecker had torn down an old house and left only a cellar hole. There was trash and junk all over the place. And it smelled in the heat. Jim wrinkled his nose as he settled cross-legged, his back against a pile of chipped bricks, and drew a deep breath of relief. Of course, disappearing would not stop *them*. He scowled. Why couldn't they just leave him alone for once? Just for once!

At least he had escaped having to go to the

beach today, but when he went back he would listen to *them* yak-yak-yak. Even now he nearly plugged his ears with his fingers just thinking of Mrs. Dale's nice, "reasonable" voice going on and on and on about how Jim must learn to make friends with other boys.

Jim's scowl grew deeper. Then Mr. Dale would take over, with talk about Little League and the Y swimming and—Jim had heard it all about a million times. While all he wanted was to be by himself. No one seemed to understand that.

He had overheard them talking about him, saying things like "brooding" and "shock." But when the whole world you had always counted on breaks up in little pieces—well, you can't just go to Cubs or Little League (he had never liked baseball anyway) as if nothing happened. You remembered, and hurt inside, and sometimes tried to believe that all the past two months were a bad dream you were going to wake up from pretty soon. There would be a pancake morning because it was Saturday and Mom had more time. Then maybe Dad would say, "How about a run out to the lake" and—

Jim wedged his fist into his mouth. He was not going to cry!

He tugged at the neck band of his Tee shirt. His skin itched there. Maybe a bug had crawled in. He made an effort to look down, though he could not see any of his neck. When he gave that up as impossible and raised his eyes again, he was no longer alone.

Jim blinked. They had lived in a town house before—before Dad and Mom had taken the plane—the plane that had crashed. And there had been no pets allowed there. Dad had always promised that when his job here was finished he would ask for a transfer and they could have a regular house and maybe a dog—

Jim chewed his lower lip. The animal facing him suddenly yawned, showing needle pointed teeth and a curling, rough-coated tongue. It was the largest and blackest cat Jim had ever seen. In the sun its fur gleamed as if each shining hair had a tiny rainbow tip. Between its green eyes there sprouted an odd, thin V-shape of white hairs, and the very tips of its four paws were also white.

The cat stared compellingly at Jim. Jim did not know very much about cats, but he did know this was no scrawny stray like the ones that usually slunk around the alley behind the Dales' house. Mrs. Dale put out bowls of water and food at times, but the animals would never come near enough to drink or eat until people left. Mr. Dale said it was wrong to encourage them, that the Animal Control should be called.

This cat was not afraid of Jim in the least, and it had eaten a lot better food than garbage scraps. Did all cats just sit and watch you this way? As if they could see into your head and know what you were thinking?

"Hello—cat—," Jim found himself talking as if to a person. He even held out his hand a little way, not quite daring to pat the head that now advanced to sniff delicately at Jim's fingers. The big cat answered with a small, polite sounding rumble.

Though he knew that the cat could not possibly understand, Jim asked questions as he would of another boy.

"You live in that apartment?" He waved towards the building on the other side of the lot. To his vast surprise, the cat moved his head from side to side as if he were saying "no!"

"Are you lost?" Jim ventured, after his shock wore off a little.

For the second time the cat shook his head. His unblinking green eyes, the pupils now

only black slits in the sun, held Jim, seeming to force the boy to return his stare.

Jim squirmed. He did not understand what was happening and he was becoming a little afraid. But he did not know how cats acted. Maybe this was the way they always met people. There were a lot of smart cats in shows on TV, like the ones that advertised cat food, and some others Jim had seen. Perhaps the alley cats were smart, too, but nobody gave them a chance to show it.

"Tiro." Jim said the word aloud. It did not sound like a name; but once more the cat rumbled, as if he were pleased with Jim. The boy was as sure that Tiro was the cat's name, as if the animal himself had said it. Though how *could* he have known?

"I'm Jim," he said, feeling a little odd as he introduced himself to a cat. "Jim Evans. And I'm staying with the Dales." He jerked a thumb over his shoulder towards the fence he had just crawled through. "I'm—they took me in 'cause I'm a foster child. My Mom and Dad —" There was a sudden lump in his throat which he could not fight. His hands doubled into fists, and he beat them into the plaster-whitened dust beyond his knees. "The court says I got to live with them—here."

6

Tiro was listening—and understanding, too. Jim could not say why he knew this or how. But it was so. And suddenly something broke, perhaps that knot in his throat, the hard feeling in his chest that had been there so long. Jim was crying and he did not care. Now Tiro moved, coming straight to him. One white-tipped paw rested on Jim's knee, and through that touch the boy could feel a vibration. He dropped his hand on Tiro's head. Now he could hear as well as feel—the cat was not rumbling, he was purring. And that purr carried with it feelings of sympathy that Jim could accept, while the best-meant words he had listened to these past weeks had only been words he did not want to hear.

The purr went on and on. Now soft fur rubbed against Jim as the big cat pressed closer to him. The boy wiped his hand across his eyes, smearing the dust on his cheeks. He felt empty, but somehow better than he had since they had told him the news about the plane crash.

"I—I like you!" Jim said shyly. He hugged the cat close. Tiro set both front paws together on Jim's chest and reached up to touch noses with the boy.

"Scat, Skoo, what'll I do—do—do"

Jim and Tiro both turned their heads. There was a little figure hip-hopping from the back alley into the waste land where Jim had taken refuge. Dirty old sneakers much too large, tied on with pieces of string, were flopping with each hop. Above those were skinny, dark brown legs. Ragged shorts of faded red clothed the upper part of those knobby-kneed legs. The shorts, in turn, were hidden by folds of a dirty Tee shirt. There was a much-faded emblem on the front of that, and what had once been long sleeves had been hacked off, their edges left to ravel. They covered very thin arms showing elbows as sharp as the knees.

"Skit, Scat, Skoo, the Devil take you—"

The newcomer was a girl. Her small head was covered by wiry black braids and surrounded a face in which large eyes were divided by a button of a nose and a wide mouth which shaped the words she sang.

Over one shoulder, a shoulder so thin and small it would seem any weight would break it in two, she carried a gunny sack, which had been patched with pieces of cloth sewn into place by big, uneven stitches. One or two threads were hanging as if it was about to come loose and let fall whatever that bumpy

8

sack contained. Setting the bag down, the little girl made a sudden dart at the pile of old boards and returned, waving two Coke bottles in triumph.

"Lucky day, sure is a lucky day!" she announced to the world at large. "Somebody leaves good cash money lyin' around—" She tucked the bottles carefully into her sack and then squatted down to inspect one of the loose patches, pulling the thread tighter and trying to tie its end fast to another dangling one.

"No good to find 'em and lose 'em," she commented. "I got to borrow a needle an' get busy, sew these up again—" She was frowning as she shifted the sack, turning it around to inspect the other side. Then for the first time she saw Jim and Tiro.

"What are you doing here, boy?" she demanded shrilly, her hands resting on her hips, her face pinching together in a scowl. "This place—I found it first, yesterday. It's *my* picking-up lot!"

Tiro slipped out of Jim's hold to trot toward the newcomer. Now he gave a small, sharp cry. The girl backed up a step.

"That's a big old cat for sure. I ain't fightin' him."

Tiro sat down as if to assure the girl he

meant no harm. With a wary glance now and then in his direction, she looked to Jim again.

"I told you, this here's my hunting ground. I ain't gonna let nobody in, neither."

Jim stood up. "You hunting bottles? What for?"

Her scowl changed to a surprised expression. "What for? 'Cause they're worth cash money, boy. How come you ask me a silly thing like that? Or," she eyed his clothing, "you rich folks don't have to worry about no money back on bottles? Anyway, you get off my place." She looked about her and then seized upon a part of an old window frame which still had a rusty nail or two on one end. She swung this warningly in his direction. "I can give you a few whacks, boy. I ain't nobody you can push around—"

"I don't want to push you around." Jim thought she had a lot of spunk. Why he was a lot bigger than she and she did not know that he would not fight her back.

"You'd better not!" She waved the piece of frame. "And you better go right back where you came from, too."

"Look here," Jim shoved his hands into his pockets. Maybe now she would understand he did not mean her any trouble. "I'm not hunting anything here. I just found this cat and—" But how could he explain what his meeting with Tiro meant to him? That was private, very private.

The girl looked toward Tiro. "He's a mighty big old cat. If he is lost someone might pay to get him back." She stared at the cat, as if she was thinking of popping Tiro into her bag along with whatever loot she might find. Though, Jim decided, she would find that rather difficult if Tiro decided not to allow it.

"He's my cat now," he said, and then knew that his words were the truth.

"You sure? Well, he'd make a big armful. Where you come from anyway?"

Jim pointed to the fence. "From over there. One of the boards is loose, I got under it."

"Courtland Place, huh. Then you don't need to sneak around taking things off *my* hunting ground." She blazed back into her one-sided quarrel again.

"I'm not," Jim began to be cross. "I don't want anything. What do you hunt?"

"Things," she returned. "Things 'at I can get money for. Granny—" For a moment her scowl slipped and Jim sensed, rather than knew, that under her will-to-battle there was fear. "Granny is took bad. She and me, we're

all the family there is. I got to get around and look for stuff so I can buy things for Granny."

"Suppose I help," Jim said impulsively. "If you tell me what you need, can't I look, too?"

Even as he asked, he felt that queer little twitch in his mind. *Tiro* wanted him to do this. But how could he know what a *cat* was thinking? It did not add up to any real sense.

For a long moment the girl hesitated before she gave a quick nod.

"All right," but she sounded grudging. "I get bottles, I get anything that can be sold. Down there—," she pointed to the hole of the old cellar, "maybe some things got left there. Nobody wants 'em now but if we look—"

Jim edged nearer to peer down into the smelly hole. There was part of a crumbling stair not too far away. He wondered if he dared trust it to hold his weight. The girl was already heading in that direction. She looked over her shoulder.

"I'm Elly, Elly Mae Brown," she announced. "And I live in Cock Alley."

"Where's that?" Jim was watching her go down the remains of the stairs. She jumped from one to the next, and did not seem to think they would slip or give way.

"Back there!" Elly waved one hand, but Jim could not be sure just which direction she was pointing toward. It did not really matter. He started down the stairs at a slower and more careful pace.

As Elly and Jim were engrossed in their hunting out in the jumble of discarded brick, junk and weed tangles, a shadow shifted. Tiro raised his black head to look coolly and critically in that direction.

Immediately the shadow froze, so quickly that one had to have very good eyes, cat eyes, in fact, to make out what sat there. It was a second cat.

"Fool!" Tiro's silent thought warning sped to the other's mind. "This is not the time nor the place to show yourself. I have made contact with the 'boy'. He is not to see the two of us together here! They have not our ease of thought, but neither are they to be underestimated."

"They seem harmless," answered the second cat.

Tiro held up his head, licking at the fur on his chest. "You have seen the history rolls! Harmless!—They are the most cruel and least logical species *we* have ever encountered."

He waited a little uneasily for the other to comment on his own sympathy with the boy. Such liking for any human, unless it was used to make that human help them, was not a part of scout training. At least Mer had sense enough not to remind him of that particular point in the manual. After all, Tiro was the senior Ka-at field operative on this mission. This was Mer's first field trip; therefore, a certain rashness might be expected.

The black cat surveyed his companion critically. He himself was the necessary one-quarter Terran breed demanded for field operatives on this world, but his magnificent appearance was more that of the pure Ka-at type. Mer's body was longer legged in proportion to her thin body. Her tail was slender as a whip lash, and her face narrowed to a more pointed muzzle. Her color was a greyish white, not much different from the drifts of dirty plaster on the ground, save that her head, legs and tail were several shades darker than the rest. She looked like one who had gone without enough food for days, and had a certain air of wildness. A very good job of make-up, Tiro thought. Mer could slink through alleys and creep into places in this tiresome city where a

Ka-at of his own fine appearance would be marked instantly, even by a short-sighted human.

"You have the orders. Two days to establish yourself, then a meeting."

"I shall take the 'girl'."

Tiro could not believe he had caught that thought clearly.

"Someone like her has no value, sister. You will only waste valuable time." He tried not to show the irritation he felt.

"Brother, I have done as we were bid. There are those in the hide-life holes she comes from who are true kin. I have already marked them; why else am I here? She came —I followed."

Tiro licked once more at his breast fur. It was for Mer to choose, and if she chose wrongly she would face the penalty. Again he half expected her to answer his thought. But when he looked up again she was gone. So at least she would follow rules and make contact with her chosen "child" at a distance.

He listened to the voices and sounds in the cellar below and settled himself to await Jim's return. Only his surface thoughts were engaged with the boy. He was really considering other, darker knowledge that had brought him to what all the ancient records of his own race proclaimed was the most violent and unhappy of worlds.

2

Tiro, Mer and Problems

"No, WE CAN'T keep that stray in the house, Jim."

"Tiro's no stray! Somebody must have lost him. Look at him, will you, just look at him? He's no stray out of the alley."

Tiro, held close in Jim's arms, his white-tipped paws on the boy's shoulders, gave one of his deepest rumbles. But the eyes he turned on Mrs. Dale were not particularly friendly. It did not really matter so much if these humans took him in or not. If he did not have this odd liking—yes, *liking*—for the boy, he would have been off and out of the house when this wrangle first started.

Jim's face flushed. Tiro was the only thing he had really wanted since the first bad days.

"Well, for a while then." Jim knew what that meant. Tiro could stick around until Mr. Dale came home. Then there would be talk about taking the cat to an animal shelter and—

"I'm going to keep him," the boy said with determination. "I've got my allowance. I can buy cat food—"

"It's more than just food," Mrs. Dale warned. "He'll have to have shots, one at least, for rabies. And those are expensive; remember that, Jim. Yes, he is a beautiful cat. But I think you are right, someone lost him. We'll have to keep watching the Lost and Found in the paper."

Jim's breath whooshed into the fur on the top of Tiro's head. At least he had won this much; she was going to let Tiro in and feed him. The boy knew that he would fight in every way he could to keep the cat. Luckily, the phone rang; and as Mrs. Dale went to answer it, Jim took the steps, mostly two at a time, to put Tiro in his room before she noticed. He set Tiro on the bed and scratched behind the cat's ears, soothed by an answering purr, as his new, fur-coated companion half closed his eyes and kneaded the bed cover with his front paws.

"Now where did *you* come from?" asked Elly. Her limp bag was slung over her shoulders. She had been down to Uncle Slim's junk yard and there was cash money tied up in a rag and stuck under her Tee shirt. She had not had to share with that boy either, though he had been the one to find all them old glass jars a-waiting on a low down shelf in the cellar hole.

Here was another big cat, not the black one the boy said he had found. And it was sitting on the doorstep watching her just like it was at home and she was only folks come visiting. Sure was a funny-looking cat, kind of two colored, and with blue eyes, *blue* eyes. Elly knew only the wild cats who ran from among the trash cans when she was hunting throw aways. This was a different sort of cat; it did not seem in the least afraid. And because it was not, Elly was—a little.

This was her doorway, the door itself hanging crooked because a lot of the wood was rotted away. Cock Alley was all shanty houses. But this was likely the worst of the lot, Elly reckoned. There was only one room inside and the windows were nothing but frames. Elly had tacked some old gunny sacks over those. Kept out the light, but kept out some of the wind and a little of the cold in winter, too.

Now the cat raised a front paw to lick the fur over its claws. Elly swung her empty bag.

"You—you go away!" she commanded. "This house is mine, mine and Granny's. We got no cats. Don't want 'em either!"

She had never seen a cat with such blue eyes which stared right into hers. Elly wiped her hand across her forehead. Sure was hot. She wished she had a popsicle, an orange one, all cool and icy. Elly had to get inside to see how Granny was doing. Granny had said she was tuckered out that morning, that she would stay in bed a little longer, just to rest her old bones. Granny had awfully old bones, and they were always hurting her now.

"Get away!" Elly flapped the bag at the cat but it did not even blink. Putting as much distance between her and the animal as she could, the girl edged around the half-open door.

It was dark inside and it smelled. But Elly was so used to both the dusky room and the smells she didn't even notice them—much. There was an old rusty wood stove by the far side, and a table which had lost part of one leg so it was propped up on a couple of bricks. On that was Granny's fry pan and two dented bowls Elly had found. Under the table was a bucket with a dipper dropped into the water it held.

"It's me, Granny!" Elly went directly to the sagging cot. "Me. I had some luck, I did. Found a lot of old jars and Uncle Slim gave me a dollar and forty-two cents." She pulled her tied-up treasure from under her shirt.

Granny's head turned on the pillow and Elly loosed a sigh of relief. Sometimes Granny just lay there and slept, not answering her at all.

"Come here, child," the voice from the bed was hardly more than a whisper. "You're a right smart one, you are, Elly. Could you just fetch me a drink of water now? It's been plenty hot—"

" 'Course." Elly ran for the dipper. Then she settled Granny's head on her arm with the ease of long practice and watched her sip once or twice. "Plenty more, Granny," she urged.

"I've plenty, Elly. That tastes right fine — for city water. Back home we had a well with the coldest, sweetest water a body ever set lip

to. That was a long time ago, a long time ago—"

"You get well, Granny, and I have some more luck like I had today, and we'll get on the bus and go there." Elly was dreaming her favorite dream, though out loud this time. Granny had told her so much about the old home place, it seemed like she had once been there herself.

The small woman on the bed pulled herself up to a sitting position, and Elly hurried to wedge a ragged quilt and stained, coverless pillows behind her.

"I got a dollar forty-two cents," the girl repeated. "And I'll go up to the supermarket. Crissie says they've got a basket by the door where they put cans that are dented a little or such. They sell them for a lot less money. I'll find you some soup, Granny, and maybe something else 'cause the bakery is on the way and they have bread that's a day old and cheaper."

"What's that, girl?" Granny looked past Elly, her wrinkled, toothless face showing surprise. "That a rat? Get the broom, Elly! Get the broom. Don't let no old rat—!"

Elly's eyes had adjusted to the gloom enough to see what was sitting on the floor near the bucket, still staring at her.

"It's no rat, Granny, it's a big cat. It was sitting right there on the doorstep when I came home, just like it owned the place! I'll get the broom and—"

But she did not want to chase the cat. There was something about the way it looked at her, as if it knew Elly Mae Brown right from her head to her heels. And it never spit, nor growled at her. With a cat around maybe Granny would not be so afraid of rats the way she was when Elly had to go out hunting sell things.

"A cat? Where did you get a cat, child? We can't feed no cat."

"Don't have to," Elly returned. "If she sets herself here long enough she'll get that big devil rat you hate, Granny. She will stay while I go and get something to eat. You don't have to be afraid."

She willed herself to prove that to Granny by reaching out her hand towards their visitor. The grey-and-white head lifted as the cat sniffed at Elly's fingers, then higher still, rubbing back and forth under her hand.

Elly was startled. The cat liked her! That was a strange thing. She was Granny's child, and one or two of the women along the Alley would give her things—like Mrs. Dabney who had given her this shirt, even cut the sleeves for her so it would fit better. But she had no friends. The children of Cock Alley went to school when the truant officer caught up with them and ran around in gangs when he didn't. Besides, Granny never wanted Elly to mix with them. Now she was too busy looking after Granny to waste time on foolishness the way the others did. But—this cat liked *her*. It gave her a new, warm feeling deep in her insides.

Jim crept down the dark stairs. Somewhere Tiro was out in the night where Mr. Dale had put him at Jim's bedtime. He had allowed Jim to fix a box in the garage, with a couple of old beach towels Mrs. Dale found, to make a bed —but said firmly no cats inside. At this moment Jim was so angry he had completely forgotten his own troubles.

There was a big police dog living with the Harrises. Jim had heard Roddy Harris boasting how his dog got cats, killed them, too. Jim had taken an early dislike to Roddy; now he felt like fighting. Suppose Rex was to get Tiro? The very thought made him shiver even though it was such a hot night. And the Harrises always turned Rex out in their yard as a guard dog. Tiro could go that way without knowing the danger.

Jim scuttled down the back hall and fumbled with the latch of the door leading into the garage. He would bring Tiro in, maybe hide him in the closet. The door gave after a strong battle with the inner bolt and Jim got in alongside of the car.

"Tiro?" he called softly. He hurried to the box but it was empty, just as he feared it would be. "Tiro?" He did not dare shout the way he wanted to; the Dales would hear him if he tried that.

Outside the moon was bright. He could hear cars going by, down at the end of the street where the highway was, and the distant cry of a police siren. Jim shifted from one slippered foot to another. He could not just go back to bed and lie there worrying about Tiro.

As quietly as he could, the boy moved out into the yard. He could hear some odd sounds which might be night things— "Tiro?"

It was as if he could see the big black cat in his mind, as clearly as if Tiro were right out there in the moonlight sitting and watching him, just as he had watched Jim at their first meeting.

Jim halted. Tiro *was* here. He put his hand

uncertainly to his head. Tiro was not lost, he had not strayed down towards the Harris house. No, Tiro knew all about such dogs as Rex, and how a cat could get hit by a car down on the highway, and—Jim swallowed. This was the queerest feeling he had ever had in his whole life! He was perfectly sure of the truth about Tiro, as sure as if—as if Dad or Mom stood right there to tell him so. And Jim could not think of anything surer than that.

Tiro was safe, he would come back. Jim was not to worry. With a big sigh of relief the boy closed the door to the garage and shot the bolt. All at once he was very sleepy and he wanted nothing so much as his own bed.

The moonlight lay in ragged patches within the waste where the house had been torn down. There were plenty of shadows for the wary to use as cover. Tiro slid from one to another with the caution of a well-trained scout. He felt relieved that he had been able to reassure Jim so easily. That the boy had been so alarmed for him surprised Tiro a little. His only other assignment on this world had been spent with a family very willing to let any "pet" attached to them go its own way at night. Tiro wondered if Jim were different from others of his kind. Then he remembered some of the stories gathered from the half-kin. There were apparently some humans who had thought for lives beside those of their own species.

The big black cat stood under the arch of an unpruned and broken-branched bush. Under his paws the dead and withered flowers of lilac were soft. He sent forth the questing thought and waited.

It was not long before Mer came. She slunk, belly low, under an arch of branch, to settle herself in the same sitting position. The tip of her tail was tucked neatly over the tips of her paws.

"You have made contact with the girl?" Tiro thought-asked.

He could sense an amusement in Mer's answer. "I am welcome—as a catcher of rats!"

Tiro could not hide his sense of disgust. That the half-kin were hunters, of course that was well known. After all they had been for thousands of years on a barbarian planet where it was necessary for them to adapt or die. But for a real Ka'at of the true line to think of hunting!

Mer's amusement grew. "Oh, I do not

chase the creatures. But a strong thought or two aimed in their direction makes them think twice about coming near. The girl—,'' Mer hesitated. "She fears for her grandmother. Also she works hard. She is not like many of the human young, thoughtless and cruel. She thinks of me as a friend."

Tiro rumbled. "When we first found this world we *were* friends of these 'men'. Our thinkers and their thinkers lived together and there was peace between us. Our wisdom fed theirs; theirs at that time enriched ours. Why, those people even believed one of our Great Ones was a goddess. They called her Bast and built temples for her in which our people lived. Then, men were glad and honored if Ka'ats chose to dwell under their roofs. But remember what followed later, sister? The dark years when their leaders said we were evil and hunted us with fire and sword, and all manner of torment? Even those who preached in new temples about a Being of Love cried out to kill when they saw us. Between us and these 'men' there now lies a river of death. We have but one duty—to liberate our kind, or those among the half-kin who are not too hardened to be reached by the inner Voice." Tiro's tail switched across the grass, his ears

31

flattened a little against his skull, and his eyes glittered.

"You sound rather like Leader Ana." Mer regarded him with her head a little on one side. Tiro found her air irritating rather than respectful. He was the Senior on this scout expedition. At least he had more experience than Mer.

"Ana knows 'man'," he replied. "You need only listen to the reports set in the ship memory banks to see how right she is. Also, we must hold by the First Directive—"

" 'Do not allow emotion to weave any tie between you and a human'," Mer repeated obediently. "Yet, we have also to keep our secret, do we not? I shall scare the rats from the girl child's house and strive to learn what I can. When is the next meeting with the Leaders?"

"I have visited the shuttle," Tiro replied. "There was no message yet on its scanner. By the way, in the boy's mind there was fear tonight of a certain dog who is encouraged to kill cats. This creature is loosed at nightfall to roam within the fence in that direction." He pointed with his chin. "Beware of him."

"It would seem that your boy thinks highly of you or he would not hold such fears in his mind.'' Mer thought-sent. ''What will happen to such as he, and this girl, when that future danger which we await strikes?''

If a cat could shrug, Tiro's movement would have been that gesture.

''They will, like the rest of their kind, get what they deserve.'' He gave the only answer expected of a self-respecting Ka'at. Yet in him there was a small, unhappy feeling. He remembered Jim's concern for him, the search the boy had made. Nonsense, one need only remember the history which lay between man and Ka'at and one could speedily forget such a silly weakness.

Mer stood up. ''It is time I began working.'' She gave a flirt of her long thin tail. ''Blest be the Great Bast and our Task.''

Tiro arose in turn. ''Walk with care, sister; this world is full of dangers.''

He watched her slide effortlessly into the shadows and then started back towards the dark bulk of Jim's house. He had already marked down a good, climbable tree. Up that and along one branch, and he could call to the boy, get through the window he had no doubt would be opened, and spend the rest of the night on a comfortable bed as befitted a Ka'at of good standing.

3

The Shadow Hangs Dark

JIM KICKED at a brick and watched it thud into the cellar hole. It was so hot and smelly down there. He would give Elly about five more minutes and then he was going. He could leave the carton right here and she would find it anyway. He glanced at the big cardboard box. Jim had lugged it all the way around the house because he could not push it under the loose board, and he was lucky no one had seen him. If Elly wanted more bottles, she sure could take her pick now.

Until he had met Elly, Jim had never really known that there was money to be made from the junk people pitched out. Oh, sure, you could take a set of Coke bottles back to the

store and get a refund. But that was different.
Mr. Dale said Jim was thoughtful to offer to
put the rubbish out for the collectors. He had
left the boy alone to sort through it. Jim found
all kinds of things for Elly: some metal frozen
food dishes, five bottles of different shapes
and sizes, and a plastic shower curtain that
had been torn off the hooks at the top and
could not be mended.

Tiro lay lazily on a pile of the old timbers.
He did not even blink as a black and yellow
butterfly went by. It had been five days since
Jim met him and there had been no notice in
the Lost and Found. Tiro was smart, Jim
thought. He let Mr. Dale put him out at night,
then a little while later he would be right up
the tree to Jim's window calling to get back
in. Tiro must be about the smartest cat ever.

Through an open window of the Dale house
came the sound of the TV. Jim shifted uncom-
fortably. Lately, the Dales had talked a lot
about the news broadcasts, the trouble in the
Middle East. All that was a long way off and
did not mean much as far as Jim was concerned. Or did it? He remembered uneasily
what Mr. Dale had mentioned once, that he
was a reserve officer and if trouble did come
he would have to join his unit. Mrs. Dale had

said something about going to her sister's place if that ever happened. And her sister lived over in Maryland on a farm. Well, if they went, Tiro could go, too. Jim was determined about that. He could get a cat carrier like the one he had seen advertised, and he would make sure Tiro was safe.

But the TV was always saying things were bad. And nothing really *did* happen, did it? Funny though, that other story the man had mentioned way at the end of his broadcast about cats disappearing in some cities. Jim watched Tiro. Who would want to take a lot of cats—not just fancy ones worth a lot of money, the kind you saw in shows, but every single cat, big or little?''

"Those old catnappers," he said fiercely to Tiro, "they won't ever get you. Why, I bet you would just tear them to pieces if they even tried it!''

Tiro was flexing his claws now, scratching at the top board of the lumber pile as if he were sharpening his natural weapons to ready himself for a fight. Jim had that odd feeling again. It had come so many times during the past five days that he wished he could tell someone about it, ask questions. He was sure Tiro understood him when he talked. Dogs, now, they understood a lot of human words like "sit" and "lie" and "stay." But those were orders. You did not give orders that way to any cat.

As Jim thought that, he saw Tiro's head turn. The cat looked toward the back of the deserted waste. A moment later Elly bobbed into view. But she was coming more slowly than she usually did, and her grin of welcome did not show at all.

"What's the matter?" Jim demanded. "Look here; they said I had to take some more stuff out for the junk man—look what I got!"

He jerked the heavy carton around. But Elly did not hurry to it as she usually did.

"Granny," she said slowly, "she's got the miseries, real bad this time. Mrs. Dabney, she said Granny ought to go to the hospital. They take Granny away and she—" Elly made a quick, fierce gesture and mopped off her face with the raveling sleeve of her old shirt. "They ain't going to take Granny! I can take care of her, just like I always have. She don't need even to be 'fraid of the rats no more when I ain't there to get the broom. They're all gone since Mer came. I can leave Granny, and Mer gets on the bed and lies real quiet, then Granny feels better, she says so!"

Mer? That was the queer-looking cat Elly had shown him once. Not handsome like Tiro, but thin and grey and white. Elly said they were friends.

"What does the doctor say?" Jim asked awkwardly. He hoped that Elly was not going to start crying.

"What doctor? We can't even get Granny to the clinic. She couldn't walk, it's a long way off. Granny, she tells me what to do. There's all kinds of plants you can use for medicine if you know them. When Granny felt better she used to go looking for 'em, and she has some dried so you can make a tea and such."

It was as if Elly lived in quite another world. Jim found it hard to believe that she could not get in a car and go to the doctor's. But what car? He had seen Cock Alley two days ago when he helped Elly carry home a carton of junk and there had been no garages there, no car except one old, battered-up truck in the street half way down with a boy working at its insides. Jim had felt strange in Cock Alley. People had stared at him, and a couple of boys made remarks he did not understand. They moved out until they seemed to block the way. But Elly had talked back with words so strange Jim did not know their meaning. Then the boys had sniggered and moved aside to let them through. But he felt that was a place he certainly would not be welcome in, alone.

"If anything happens—" Elly's breath caught, and she paused for a moment before she added, "if anything happens to Granny, I'm going to the home place. Me and Mer, we won't wait around for no welfare that wants to put me in a home and maybe give Mer to the animal catcher!"

She dropped down beside the carton and ran her hand listlessly over the shower curtain Jim had put on top. But she was not looking at that at all, but rather was staring across the old cellar hole at something which made her small face look thin and pinched. Elly was afraid and her fear spread to Jim.

He shifted awkwardly from one foot to the other. If anything happened to her granny! Well, something *had* happened to Mom and Dad—quick and bad, and with no warning at all!

"They—you might get put in a foster home," he said slowly. "Like me—"

"Never, no way!" Elly shook her head determinedly. "I ain't going to be shoved around by folks because they don't know what to do with me. I tell you, me and Mer, we're going to the home place, Granny's own home place!''

''Where's that—?''

It was like opening a door on a packed closet. Elly's words tumbled out so fast, and mixed together so, that Jim had to guess at a lot. But it was plain Elly believed that somewhere there was a wonderful house with fields all around it, and a well of clear, cold water. Bushes were so full of berries that no one could ever pick them all, and there were things to eat just growing, corn, and apples off trees. Granny had lived there before her husband got a job in the city. But it was still there, waiting—

''Do you know how to get there?''

''There's a bus that goes. Granny and me, we planned how, if we ever got enough money to buy tickets, we'd go. I have it wrote down—the name of the place the bus stops at. Granny—''

Elly suddenly bent over the carton and hid her face on the shower curtain as her words became sobs. She cried wildly so her whole thin, small body shook.

Out of the shadows stole Mer. Flitting to

the child's side, she rubbed back and forth against her, her throbbing purr loud enough for Jim to hear. Now and then the cat lifted her head and rubbed her nose against the small portion of Elly's cheek that was visible. Jim squatted down unhappily. Part of him wanted to run away; another part of him wanted to tell Elly how sorry he was, but he could not find the words. He could only watch as Elly's arm went out and gathered Mer to her in a grip that must have squeezed the cat too tightly, but there was no change in Mer's purr.

Elly's choking sobs lessened. At last she raised her head, cuddling Mer against her. She hiccupped as she said: "I ain't ever been a crybaby. Granny always said I had my head screwed on right and tight, and could make my way. And I'm going to do that!" She stared at Jim fiercely as if she expected him to deny it.

"I guess you will, Elly. I guess you can do about anything you set out to."

Elly nodded so that her braids flip-flopped. "So I ain't going to cry again. Now," she loosed Mer and turned her attention to the box Jim had dragged there, "let's get a look at all this."

Though there were the smears of tears on her cheeks, she was now the Elly he knew, and he felt more comfortable as she raked out his finds, commenting on each as she went.

There was no moon tonight and the clouds hung heavy. Tiro was pleased as he slipped into the back alley and sounded the call. Within seconds Mer joined him.

"There should be a message tonight. Our plan has begun in the west. Already even the humans, concerned as they are with their own affairs, notice. There was more news about stolen or strayed cats on their noisy television tonight."

"If the ingathering has started, then the news about this world must be grave." There was something troubled about Mer's return, as if she were worried.

"You have passed the word among the half-kin, of course?"

She did not even answer that and he deserved her snub. But the uneasiness he could sense in her made him curious. However, he did not try to break thought silence again as they padded together through the night, slid sleekly under a fence, and found their way, by a path hidden for months from humans, into an open patch in the midst of a thick circle of shrubs.

Tiro threw back his head and uttered a small, sharp call. Part of the shadowy bulk in the middle of the clearing changed shape and showed, outlined by the dimmest of lights, an opening. The black cat sprang for that small door, followed by Mer.

Once inside he stretched luxuriously. There a soft springy thickness under his feet and the greenish light were welcome to his eyes, which sometimes found the bright glare of this sun unpleasant. He paced around the small cabin, sniffing, making sure that their craft had not been invaded.

The inner core of the space shuttle was covered with thick quilting and had straps for a Ka'at to wriggle into at take off. While facing the pilot's position, there was a board across which flickered dim lights, below those, the various levers fashioned to answer to Ka'at thought.

But the one main light on the board was not flickering. Rather it beamed steadily in a brighter green. Tiro, seeing it, stiffened. The signal to report to base ship! His tail twitched in answer to the need for caution and also haste. Mer was already fitting herself under the floor straps, preparing to relax, leaving the piloting of the flyer up to him this time.

Tiro worked into his own position, watching the board intently. There was no warning that anything human was within too close a range. He thought out the right command for take off.

They were space borne almost before he expelled another deep breath, the speed of their rising pressing them down upon the carpeting. Tiro kept a careful eye on the control panel. Once aloft, they were liable to be sighted, or picked up by the humans' radar. That did not mean any great danger, for their scout craft could outrun or dodge any sky ship men yet owned, but it was always better not to be noticed.

He was not sure that they had gotten cleanly away until they were well above the lanes where even the jets traveled. Mer's eyes were closed. Her brain pattern said that she slept, after the logical Ka'at fashion, for all the responsibility of this trip was his alone.

A summons to the command ship was of utmost importance. Tiro's tail still twitched a little as he listed in his mind the many emergencies which might have arisen, though there was no use wasting time guessing which. It would be made very clear in due time.

His thoughts went to Jim. He wondered what the boy would say if he ever knew the real Tiro. Would the boy believe in a thinking Ka'at at all? Humans seemed always to wish to forget or laugh away anything that did not match their own opinions. To them a Ka'at and a cat were one and the same thing. The knowledge that a species so unlike their own had had space travel for thousands of *their* years, discovering their own rather unimportant world when men were hardly more than primitive cave dwellers, would hurt their pride so that they would instantly close their minds to such an idea and utterly deny its possibility.

As he had reminded Mer, it had not always been so. Tiro remembered taped records of the hot, desert-bordered land across the sea (the land men now called Egypt), where Ka'at and man had met, if only briefly, as honest and equal friends. Then his own people had been *too* trusting, established themselves too well, believing that man could think logically always and not be swept by storms of emotion.

So there had been many of their kind who had found this planet good, had come to live here and raise their families. Then, when the land had been overrun by war, the Ka'ats had been trapped in terror, fear and death. After that there had arisen different parties among the Ka'ats themselves.

Some had withdrawn, found other worlds to live on in peace. They had said that true logic meant there could be no more contact with this world at all, that those of their kin who remained here must be forgotten. And for a time those believing that had been in power.

But there was always the need for discovery, the one trait that Ka'ats seemed to share with man himself. Lately they had spread again into this part of the galaxy and, with that spreading, the second party had come into power.

Man was fast pushing toward disaster. He might soon vanish in one of his outpourings of violent emotion, or poison his own world. But there were still the ancient kin, enslaved in part, hunted in part, captive. So the Ka'at explorers had made *the* plan. Those of the kin who were not too far changed to receive Ka'at thought were to be brought away. Such strangers would introduce a new and vigorous strain into the ancient Ka'at kind. The long years of their exile had bred in them new traits which the Ka'ats lacked. Only the Elders on the mother ship were pure Ka'at now. Tiro and his kind had the stranger's strain in them as an experiment.

Now the time was growing very short. Tiro could guess that the news must indeed be dark if the evacuation he had heard of was already in progress. How long before man tried to kill his world? Months, by the way he himself measured time, weeks—or perhaps—days? Maybe they would know this very night.

4

The Last Order

THE SCOUT shuttle fitted itself neatly into a
hollow on the outer rim of the big headquarters ship. At the warning "ping", which announced they had reached the end of their
flight, Tiro and Mer freed themselves from
their safety straps and trotted into the other
space vessel. They hurried down a narrow
corridor and came out in the large cabin
within.

A little of Tiro's usual high self-confidence
had oozed away. Here he was not in the least
a Senior Ka'at. Rather he was a very young
and junior crew member, not to mind-send
any suggestions unless he was singled out to

do so. He settled beside Mer at the very edge of the assembly and made ready to listen.

Occupying one of the padded cushions at the very center of that gathering was Leader Ana. And beside her sat Fledyi. Tiro's whiskers lifted when he sighted Fledyi, the Senior of all Seniors. He was closer to the ideal of Ka'at than any other Tiro had ever seen.

His coat was neither yellow, nor brown-red, but a shade between the two. Even in the greenish light of the big ship, the fur shone as if each hair were spun of some precious metal. His great eyes were piercing green. He was larger than any other male among them; and his tail lay across the edge of the cushion grandly, like a banner he might raise at any moment to urge them to action.

Ana lay more at ease. Her fur was a silver grey, but she also had the green eyes of pure Ka'at blood. Now those eyes swept back and forth across the company, marking each of them in turn. Tiro was glad that he and Mer were not the last to come. Two more scouts padded in breathlessly, settling down beyond them.

"Good voyage," Ana's thought swept out in a greeting suitable for Senior to Juniors.

"The work goes well, but it must be hastened. Listen to Fledyi and learn why."

"There is but little time left, brothers, sisters," Fledyi's round, unblinking eyes also swept over them, catching each in a stare which he held for perhaps the length of a single breath. "The humans move faster than we had hoped. I, myself heard councils of those who plan a surprise attack on their own kind. Of such are the humans! They purr when facing one another, unsheathing claws the while. The sooner they are gone from time and space, the better will be the future for all other life forms. But we still have our task. Ana has set the far-signal and received answer. There are ten ships on the way, already well into the border of this solar system. So our brothers and sisters of the forgotten ones must be ready to enter them. Since even ten ships will be small for our cargo, we shall send the half-kin off in the deep sleep. They will need no nourishment, nor any room save for a resting body, while they remain in space. I do not know how many we can take even with this arrangement."

Ana stirred. "We must take all who answer our summoning!"

Her thought sped like a fierce raking of unsheathed claws. "They are our kin; should they be left here to suffer for what man has done?"

Mer watched Ana, cloaking her own thought. Were all humans as evil as she had been taught? Surely some of their young might be considered harmless, even a little trustworthy. Elly had shared her own soup with Mer last night, even though the Ka'at knew that the girl had been hungry enough to eat it all. And in the far past, had not Man and Ka'at lived in peace together? Could not they, the good ones, be warned of the evil to come?

She was suddenly startled at her own thoughts. No Ka'at could trust a human. They might be interesting, even enjoyable at a young age, but when grown— One merely had to consult the records, gaze at what they had done to their own world, to know what the creatures were really like. She must watch herself, remember always true Ka'at logic.

Tiro's tail tip twitched. So perhaps the end of this human trouble was coming even faster than they had first thought. He knew the reports, had seen and heard tapes other scouts had brought back. Humans had built huge death machines and were ready to use them.

Maybe one of their cities could vanish in a rain of fire. Or worse, their kin within it could be killed by a poison in the air. There was this wildness in man—and it was also in some of the half-kin—that he was never content with what he had, but wished to take that of his kin, or even make that kin a servant to him, even as Ka'ats had servants of machines. But Ka'ats ruled the machines, not their own kind.

One part of his mind listened and filed away Leader Ana's instructions concerning the need for the faster summoning and transportation of the half-kin. He heard Fledyi say again in warning that the time was very short. Well, he and Mer would set the signal as soon as they got back to their station. Any half-kin with enough Ka'at left in him or her to respond to the kin summons would come. They could ferry many on board the scout shuttle itself and when the other ships came they could—

Jim. Tiro did not know why he now saw Jim in his mind. The boy was merely human, to be used by Tiro to protect his own mission. Jim had been a key Tiro had turned to get into a centrally placed house, one from which he could operate successfully. Generations of humans had used cats and other beings for less 'humane' purposes.

Yet the Ka'at felt uncomfortable. Almost, now, he could feel Jim's fingers scratching behind his ears, hear the boy talking. A lot of human nonsense, of course, about how handsome Tiro was and all that. Maybe if a human were young enough—

Tiro realized suddenly that Leader Ana was regarding *him*. He was wondering if he had been send-thinking stupidly. She was staring at him so intently that he could feel the force of her send-think pushing against his mind. Somehow she must have guessed, or felt, that his attention had strayed. Such was not right, for a scout! He was no cubling.

Now Leader Ana arose to her full height, matching Fledyi, as if her silver-grey formed a shadow for his brilliant gold.

"What is the First Law of a scout?" Her mind flashed out that question as a tail might lash in fury.

There was a stir among the listening Ka'ats. Tiro could sense their surprise. Ana waited for no reply from them. She herself stated that First Law in almost instant response to her question: " 'The Ka'at is Ka'at, he shall give kin-closeness to none not of his own blood.' "

Tiro's tail tip moved. It was too close an answer to his idle speculation of a few moments before. Somehow—somehow Ana must have guessed! Then he became aware of Mer's shifting. She gave forth the feeling of a small cubling caught in the midst of some illogical misdeed. Mer? Was Ana really looking at his companion rather than himself? He had warned Mer; he would make it very plain when they were together again where such foolishness could lead.

"Remember," Ana continued, "these humans cannot be trusted. They are not the same as those who welcomed us once to their world. To these we are lesser beings to be played with and then thrown away when the human tires. There is no kin-blood between us. Let no foolish liking for any touch us. If they pull down their world, they do it knowingly and because of the evil in their hearts. What comes to them now grows from a seed which they planted; it has no part in our lives. Long ago our Leaders made a mistake when they came to this world because they thought these creatures could be friends, equal to us. Leaders had found some among them who could indeed be taught to send-thought. But as men learned what they might do, their pride and their greed grew greater and greater. Their Leaders did not tell them that they were only one of many life forms who must learn to dwell together on a single world, learning peace and sharing with each other. No, their pride-filled Rulers said that the world and all within and without it belonged to them, and with it they could do as they pleased. They could give death at will, even to their own kin. This is how they have lived and now they may die."

It was the truth, Tiro agreed. All Ka'ats knew that truth. The humans made the ugliness which in the end probably would overcome and destroy them. And he thought-heard agreement from all who listened.

But it was Fledyi who then interrupted. "Humans are rightly no business of ours. Think, Ka'ats, of our kin. Go now to your assigned places and set the call beacons. Your time may be very short and this is the duty laid upon you."

Mer said nothing as she settled into her harness and Tiro piloted the shuttle away from the ship. There were all the others flitting out, speeding to their own districts. Tiro set the course and made ready to pick up any hint that they might be observed at their earth landing place.

"The humans' war is very terrible."

Mer surprised him with her sudden comment.

"You have seen the record tapes. They always learn of worse weapons to be used."

"But there are humans who speak out against such weapons, try to stop these wars. That, too, is in the records."

"A very few. And those the rest turn upon and call non-kin," Tiro reminded her.

"It is a pity. There is some good in them. Surely that can be reached. True, they are lesser than Ka'at—perhaps because they cannot think-send. If they could ever be one mind at times, as we are one mind, then this wildness in them might be tamed. If they could once think-send, why did that power depart from them?"

Tiro was proud of his own knowledge of the tapes. "As Leader Ana said to us, there were never more than a few who could do this. And even then there were wars and killings. It is said in one such war those who dwelt in the teaching house of Bast were slain, and none thereafter could meet us mind with mind. No longer did the humans know what once we both had. Then there came strangers who did not even possess the memory of Bast. Those took our kin away to strange places where they had to hunt their food, to learn to kill to eat.'' Tiro shuddered. ''Our kin forgot their high blood, lost some of their gifts, but never did they surrender in spirit to Man or call him master. And this, too, was held against us by humans who must rule all.''

''Some humans have little for themselves,'' Mer commented.

''Sharing is not of their nature.''

''That is not always so. The girl Elly shares.''

Tiro turned his head. ''Sister, remember the First Law. We have our mission. It might be well for you not to seek out that human child again.''

''Say as well for yourself, brother,'' Mer's thought snapped back. ''Is the boy Jim so old in evil that you hate him? I have watched you. He may not touch minds so well with you, but how else did he know your name? You must have tried the thought-send with him.''

''That has never been forbidden,'' Tiro defended himself. ''We make use of that talent to establish a contact when we are pressed for time. It is not real thought-send for it is never clear.''

He caught Mer's amusement and felt angry.

He had been far too quick to reply, as if he were ashamed of how he had caught Jim's attention. Yet it was all very proper and what any Ka'at scout would have done. They had discovered long ago that many of the children of humans were far easier to reach than the adults. And it was a standard rule to first approach a child when one needed a base.

He closed mind. If Mer wanted to be foolish, then let her. After all, their stay here would be short. They had been given the last order. From now on they would have only one duty, the collecting and directing of those of the kin who could be reached, the evacuation of a threatened world.

Jim awoke. It was very early in the morning and there was no black shape curled at the foot of his bed. Now he remembered Tiro had not mewed outside the window last night, had never come to be let in. Some of the same uneasiness which had attacked him the first time the big cat had disappeared returned. Rex, and the highway, and all the many bad things that could happen to unwary cats prowling the night were only too easy to remember. He could not just lie there and wait.

The boy dressed hurriedly. Luckily, it was

vacation and he did not have to go to school. As he opened his bedroom door, he heard the phone ring, loud in the lower hall, more muffled in the bedroom. Then it stopped. One of the Dales must have answered. Tiro—! No, nobody was going to call this early about a cat. And hardly anyone knew Jim had him anyway. He tried to reassure himself all the way down to the kitchen.

Unlocking the back door he stepped out into the open. It felt cool this early, but it would not take long for the day to get muggy. How did Elly manage? That awful old room down in that nasty place; it must be as hot as an oven. And what would happen to Elly if they sent her granny off to the hospital? He believed her when she said she would run off if she were left alone. Elly was like Mer, like Tiro. Jim could not imagine anyone making either the girl or the cats do what they did not want to do.

Over the fence leaped a black furred body.

"Tiro!" Jim's voice was full of relief. "Where've you been, old boy?"

The cat rubbed back and forth around his bare ankles and he dropped down to hug him. Tiro only allowed this for a second or two before he wriggled determinedly free and started for the house, looking back and mewing an order to hurry. It was breakfast time for all logical beings.

Jim fed the cat and then dumped dry breakfast food into a bowl. He was trying to decide whether he should slice a banana over it when Mr. Dale came through the swinging door.

"Jim? Oh, good, you're up. I have to leave early. Tell Margaret I'll get a cup of coffee on the way and phone her as soon as I have any news." For a moment he hesitated, as if he were going to add something. Jim moved guiltily between him and Tiro. Maybe he was going to begin again about not feeding "that animal" in the house. "Listen, don't you worry," Mr. Dale was watching him, not looking for the cat. "We arranged everything. If Margaret leaves, you'll go on with her to Maryland. You'll like it there; it's a lot better than the city in summer. So long—"

He swung back through the door before Jim could answer. So they were really planning to go to Maryland. Jim thought of his bank upstairs—did he have enough to buy the cat carrier? If he did not, maybe he could hunt up some bottles and things to sell. This time not to help Elly but because he sure needed the money himself. He shoved aside the banana and began to chomp down the cereal as fast as he could. Tiro usually took a morning nap. All right, he would shut him up in the patio room so he could not go off if Jim had to find him in a hurry.

Maybe he could call up some stores and ask about the price of carriers. Jim chewed faster and faster as he tried to think ahead.

5

"Going to Find Us
a Home Place—"

THERE WAS nothing interesting or useful in the small amount of trash that had been collected in the bin lately. Jim made only a pretense of poking into it a job he had to force himself to do. He had five dollars in his bank, that he had made sure of before he left the house. But the on-sale carrier cost twice that, if the store still had one left.

Elly might be happy with nickels and dimes, but Jim had to do better than that, and in a very short time, too. Mrs. Dale had told him the truth when she had come down before Jim left the house. Mr. Dale's early morning call had been from the reserve officer's head-quarters. He was being called back to duty. Then Mrs. Dale had turned on the small radio in the kitchen and there had been a lot of talk about trouble overseas which Jim hardly listened to, being far more absorbed in the idea of getting the cat carrier.

"I'll phone Elizabeth tonight," Mrs. Dale snapped off the radio before the announcer had finished. Her face looked queer, as if she was scared. "It won't take long to close things up here. Maybe we can take off the same day Robert leaves."

But, Jim remembered, she had not said what day that would be. How much time did he have? Hi—there was a Coke bottle! He picked it up out of the gutter. Yes, it was not broken and he could take it back— for pennies. It would take more than one Coke bottle to get what he needed.

He did not squeeze through the fence to reach the lot where the house had been. This time he slipped around the boards the workmen had left in front. Jim was sure Elly had pretty well combed the cellar for anything salable, but he would just look again.

Jim had reached the head of the steps when he heard a sound which stopped him short. At first he thought it was some kind of animal that had been hurt and was calling for help.

He hurried toward the pile of old lumber. It sounded as if it came from behind there.

As he rounded the boards he saw her.

"Elly!" Jim skidded to a stop.

She had her arms clasped about her shins, her head bent over so all he could see was her hair, nothing of her face at all. But it was Elly making those strange sounds! Beside the girl's shoulder Mer rubbed her head back and forth, now and then adding a little cry of her own.

"Elly, what is the matter?" Something terrible must have happened. In all the time Jim had known Elly he had never seen her like this. He reached out his hand and touched her arm anxiously.

"—go—way—!" The words were so muffled he could hardly understand. The girl hunched her shoulders as if to throw off both his touch and Mer's.

Elly must be sick. Jim glanced around the overgrown garden of the vanished house. Should he go and get Mrs. Dale? He felt very useless. But he had never mentioned Elly to the Dales.

"Are you sick?"

Now that he looked more closely he could

see a big bag lying beside her, stuffed full, with a piece of old rope tied around to keep it shut. Jim recognized what made the bag itself. That was the quilt from Granny's bed!

"Elly," Jim's voice wavered; he did not want to ask this question but he knew that he must. "Elly, has something happened to Granny?"

It was as if he had stuck her with a knife. Her head jerked up so he could see her wet cheeks, her eyes nearly swollen shut with crying.

"Granny's gone—" she wailed. "They came an' took her to the hospital. Then the doctor—he told Mrs. Bagley that she was dead— And then—I just—I just run. I got my things," she patted the bundle beside her, "and I run— 'fore they come to get me! I got a dollar. But that ain't near enough to take Mer and me to the country. So we got to find us a place where we can hide out 'til I find us enough to go. But Granny—" Her mouth began to quiver again and her words ended in a wail. She clutched blindly at Jim, ramming her head against his shoulder as she started to cry again.

Jim closed his eyes. He had that awful lost feeling once more, the one he had almost forgotten. As if he were back at school that day they called him out to tell him what had happened to Mom and Dad. Now it had happened to Elly, too.

At first he wanted to shove her away, to get up and run as fast as he could so that he would not have to listen to her, and remember for himself. During one bad moment he longed to shut Elly up, so he would not have to think about those things that made him feel sick inside.

But he could not do that to Elly because he knew just how she was feeling right now. Instead he held on to her almost as tightly as she was holding him, and Mer rubbed against them both, giving those small, soft calls.

Elly moved, drew away, smearing the back of her hand across her puffed eyelids.

"No use taking on this way. Granny would say use the good sense the Lord give you, girl! And that I got to do. I'll just find a place where Mer an' me can hide out 'til I get the money. Then we'll go away where no Welfare is gonna find us!"

Sniffing, she looked around, as if hunting her safe place near where she now crouched. Then she reached out and ran a hand along the boards.

"Looks like those men who smashed up this place are taking a long time gettin' back to clean up. Maybe I can make a place right here."

She got to her feet, her chin set deteminedly and shifted one of the top boards from the pile. "See here—you set this up just like this, sorta leaning it over. Then we put some others next it, and it looks like it fell off by itself, only I've got a good old place underneath to hide."

She was right. Jim, glad to be doing anything rather than listen to Elly cry, helped. Elly stood back as each board was placed to examine the result.

"Just so it looks like it did all this of itself," she said. " 'Course there ain't been any one hanging around here, but you can't never be sure. Now let's see."

Down on her knees again, she wriggled into the lean-to, pushing the quilt-wrapped bundle ahead of her. A moment later she stuck her head out again to say, "It'll do—for now."

"But what if it rains? And it gets awfully dark here at night."

Elly shrugged. "If it rains I'll set out a pot and get some water. Dark nights—" she hesitated. "I got Mer. They say cats can see in the

dark, better then folks. Mer, she'll let me know if there's any one comin'. Mer, she's a good friend.'' Elly stooped and caught up the lean grey and white cat, hugging her tight. Mer allowed this, butting her head against Elly's chin. "Say, does that big old cat of yours talk—sorta inside of your head?''

Jim was startled. "Talk? Inside my head? What do you mean?''

Elly, he could see, was entirely serious. "Well, it's this way. Mer, she looks at me sometimes real careful, then suddenly I know what she's thinkin'.'' Elly put down the cat and rubbed her own forehead. "I ain't never had a cat before, so maybe all cats do that— if folks know 'em. That true?''

Jim shook his head. "I don't know.'' Did Tiro talk to him? How had he known Tiro's name? And that time when he had been so afraid, when the black cat had wandered off, and then out of nowhere he had known everything was all right and Tiro would come home safe.

But thinking of Tiro made him remember his own problems. What about the move to Maryland, and getting a cat carrier so Tiro would not be left behind? Though now here was Elly, too. Somehow Jim could not go off and leave Elly lying under some dirty old boards in this lot, just hoping to get away to a place she had only heard stories about.

"Listen," he squatted down on his heels so he was facing Elly, "maybe I'll have to go away. The Dales—I live with them—Mr. Dale has been called back into the Army, and Mrs. Dale says she is going to Maryland to live with her sister and I have to go, too."

Elly's small face was without expression. "Don't need to think 'bout me!" she announced explosively, as if she could read Jim's mind as well as Mer's. "I can get along by my own self just fine! Me n' Mer, we'll manage just fine."

"You can't," Jim answered bluntly. "How do you know they won't be here tomorrow with a bulldozer or something to rip this place apart? Being a foster child isn't bad, really, Elly. They are kind." He was willing to admit now that the Dales had been kind.

But Elly shook her head. "Not gettin' mixed up with no Welfare, I ain't. They won't take Mer—"

The cat had seated herself before Elly, glancing from the girl to Jim and back again as if she understood every word they were saying. In fact, Jim had a touch of that old uneasiness. As Elly had said, there was something stirring within his mind. Part of him knew that Elly's choice was not right, but there was a strange other thought that argued that she was.

"I'll get you something to eat. Did you have any breakfast?" he asked, trying to shut off that stir dimming his thoughts.

"I had a little cornbread at Mrs. Bagley's," she admitted. "Seems like I couldn't eat good then—"

"You wait, I'll get you something!" Jim felt better acting than just sitting talking. He hurried to squeeze through the board in the fence and reach the kitchen. There was a murmur of a voice—Mrs. Dale was talking on the hall phone. He hoped she would not finish soon. Swiftly he took bread, spread slices thickly with peanut butter and then heaped on generous spoonfuls of jelly. There were Cokes and he got the one nearest on the shelf. Half of an open box of cookies was tipped into a sandwich bag easily enough. He thought of Mer, too, filling a second bag with dry cat food. All the time he kept listening for Mrs. Dale. There was no reason he could not help himself to a snack. The only rule was he must clean up after himself if he did. Now he sloshed the knife and the jelly spoon through water and dried them before he took off, his supplies crowded into a used grocery bag.

Tiro was ahead of Jim as he crawled through the fence again. Mrs. Dale must have let him out. Jim called to him, but the cat melted into the untamed bushes on the other side and vanished. Jim kept on to the lean-to, and pushed the bag at Elly.

"This is all I could get now. I'll try again tonight," he promised.

Elly surveyed the offering. "Boy, you sure do use the knife heavy in the jar when you spread yourself something! But that looks as good as chicken in a pot!" She held a sandwich with one hand, and with the other she carefully opened the bag of cat food. "Mer— now where did that old cat go? She was right here a minute ago. Well, she can get herself filled up when she comes back."

Elly bit into the sandwich, while Jim pried off the cap of the Coke bottle so she could drink.

"That was good!" Elly had wolfed down both of the sandwiches, but the cookies she tucked back in her bundle. "You eat mighty fancy. I ain't had a feed like that for long—"

"I'll get you more," Jim promised. He still

79

thought Elly could never make her plans come true, but he knew he did not have the force to argue with her. Maybe a couple of nights, even one, in this place would make her see that she could not go it on her own, no matter how much she was determined to do so.

Tiro watched from a place well screened by the overgrown bushes.

"See," he assured his companion in that hiding place. "The child will be all right, the boy will look after her."

"Have you mind-touched him this morning?" demanded Mer.

"Not yet."

"Then you do not know. The boy is going away. The humans with whom he lives are changing their den-place. He is determined to take you with him, because he fears for your fate if you are left."

Tiro stared. "My fate? But—"

"You and I know there is no reason for alarm. The boy does not. He sees you as denless, perhaps taken up by those humans who kill unwanted animals. He is full of fear for you!"

"I have not encouraged him," he answered.

"Perhaps not, brother. But the boy has taken you into his liking. If he were not human I would say he has claimed kinship."

"And the girl?" Tiro retorted, not wanting to believe what Mer said.

"She has claimed kin with me."

"You cannot—," Tiro was beginning, when Mer turned her blue eyes full upon him. There was that in her stare which surprised and jolted him.

"You have set the signal?" She changed the subject so sharply that he was forced to, also.

"Yes, for several shuttle trips all ready." Tiro was more than a little proud. "Tonight we open that place wherein the humans keep the homeless—that which you have spoken of. There are several therein with whom I have made good contact. We can unlatch their cages from the outside."

"Well, enough. I shall be ready."

Mer said no good-bye but slid from under the bush, heading back toward the lean-to.

Jim hated to leave Elly. He was lucky; Mrs. Dale was so occupied with her own affairs, and with what she considered Jim's future, that she was paying little attention to him here and now. Later in the afternoon he had been able to smuggle out a piece of cold ham, some more peanut butter sandwiches, and a bottle of water before she noticed that he was gone. But she was waiting for him when he returned.

"Where have you been?" There was a sharper note in her voice than there had ever been before.

"Out in the yard looking for Tiro," which was the truth, for the big cat had disappeared again. Jim was more and more worried. If Tiro was going to keep on doing that, it could happen when they were ready to leave. And he did not think Mrs. Dale would wait for him to hunt up any cat. Also he had done nothing about the carrier.

"Jim, some cats are wanderers. They settle in a place for a few days and then go again. Elizabeth has a collie. You'll enjoy him. Don't worry about Tiro."

He knew better than to protest now. All he could do was to hope the cat was around when he had to leave. Then, carrier or no carrier, he would take Tiro with him. Jim did not know what made the cat so special to him, he only knew that Tiro *was* special, that he meant more now to Jim than anyone had since Mom and Dad had gone. Unless it was Elly. And if they left he would have to do something about

Elly, too. Would the five dollars he had buy Elly the ticket to her home place? He was doubtful if it was a real place—now. The farm might have been all built over or something since Elly's granny left. Jim only knew that he could not leave Elly without anyone to know or care what became of her.

Through the dusk padded Tiro and Mer; behind them followed five other cats. They had thought-gathered these into action. At present there was only one need—to release the kin and see them to safety.

6

Jim and Elly in Search

WIND SWEEPING against the side of the house awakened Jim. Then came heavy rain. The boy sat up in bed. Elly! This was a storm, a bad one. He cowered as lightning flashed, and there was a crash of thunder so loud overhead it might have been the whole roof of the house tumbling in on him. He could not leave Elly out there with only a few old, rotten looking boards to cover her!

Crawling out of bed, shivering every time thunder roared, Jim pulled on the clothes he had left in a muddle on the chair. Tiro? Tiro had not come back either!

He had a flashlight somewhere. After a

hasty search of a top drawer his hand closed around it. There was another crack of thunder, making Jim drop the flashlight and cover his ears. Then he forced himself to pick it up and go on into the hall.

There was a dim light on downstairs, which meant Mr. Dale had not come home yet. But the other bedroom door was shut, and Jim hoped Mrs. Dale was asleep. He went down the staircase one slow step at a time.

The pound of rain was so heavy he could hear it even through the walls of the house. What could Elly do?

Jim unlatched the door into the garage. He had stopped long enough at the downstairs coat cupboard to get his raincoat and drag Mrs. Dale's from its hanger. It would be far too big for Elly, but it would give her some protection.

Outside, the rain was a solid wall. Water splashed down over the outer door of the garage. Jim shone the light into Tiro's box. There was no round black shape inside. He hesitated as another flash of lightning split the sky, followed by frightening noise.

Staying here was not going to help Elly any, yet Jim hated to venture on out into the heavy rain. He bundled the flashlight as well

as he could into the folds of Mrs. Dale's coat. It beamed out what seemed a very small glow of light, which was quickly swallowed up by the gloom before him.

The yard looked so different, Jim was not quite sure which direction to take to find the loose fence board. Finally he decided to try to get into the vacant lot from the front. There were trees in the backyard and he had heard that lightning sometimes hit trees. He ducked his head as far as he could into his collar and splashed through the water running down the drive.

Just as he reached the sidewalk, all the street lights went out. The power was off, and his muffled flashlight gave him hardly any light at all. But Jim made himself go on.

Somehow he got under the boards set to face the street and moved ahead slowly, not wanting to run into any of the piles of bricks or worse, maybe fall into the cellar hole. The thunder rolled again, but this time it sounded farther away. Jim hoped that meant the storm was passing.

His light caught the end of the board pile in its beam. Maybe Elly had had sense enough to go back to Cock Alley when the rain started.

But if she had not, then Jim must take her back to the house, no matter what she said.

"Elly?" The boards were still standing to form the lean-to. Jim flashed his light into their shadow.

There was something there. Elly had made a ball of herself within the quilt, now soaked in big dark patches. She peered out and then moved as if she would squeeze out of the other end of the lean-to.

"Elly—it's me—Jim!"

Elly's crab-crawl stopped. But what he could see of her face was not welcoming.

"Elly, look here—," Jim untangled Mrs. Dale's coat and held it out. "Put this on and come out! You can't stay out here now!"

"I ain't comin'." She shook her head with such determination that the flap of quilt she had pulled up for a hood bounced off her tangled hair. "You tell anybody I'm here, boy?" She shot the question at him as she might have thrown a stone. "Where'd you get that coat?"

"It's Mrs. Dale's. No, I didn't tell anybody you were here," Jim snapped back. He had come out in the middle of this flood to rescue Elly and just see how silly she was being. He had a mind to walk right back in the house and let the rain wash her away. "You can't stay here," he pointed out, "you might even slide down into the cellar hole—"

"Where should I go then? With you? Then that Mrs. Dale you live with, what does she do? Come mornin' she'll be on the phone to the Welfare and I'll be caught. You ain't no friend of mine, not if you want me to do that."

"You can't stay here!" Jim yelled out his irritation, repeating himself far more forcefully this time. "You're plain crazy."

He was getting soaked himself, in spite of the raincoat. Water plastered his hair to his head, rolled in regular streams down his face and neck, in under the collar. And his feet felt as if he had about a gallon in each shoe.

"I can do just what I please," Elly returned stubbornly. "You ain't giving me no orders, boy!"

"Nobody has to know," Jim could not just go away and leave her no matter how mad he was right now at her. "Mrs. Dale's sleeping, and Mr. Dale isn't home yet. They won't know about you. What about Mer?" he thought of the cat suddenly. "I'll bet she doesn't like it out in the wet."

"Mer ain't here," Elly said flatly. "That's one reason why I ain't going nowhere either. She come back an' I'm gone an' maybe I'll never find her again."

"At least take this," Jim was near to giving up, but he pushed Mrs. Dale's coat at the girl. "It'll keep you a little dryer."

"And how are you goin' to tell what became of it come morning an' the lady wants it herself?" Elly countered.

"I'll think of something—," Jim was beginning, when he was aware of something else. The rain had slackened off. There were no more lightning flashes and the thunder muttered only in the distance. He also saw in the beam of the flashlight that Elly was unwinding herself from the thickness of the sodden quilt and coming out of the lean-to. He drew a deep breath of relief. Now he would have to think about how he could get her into the house and hide her for the rest of the night, then let her out in the morning before the Dales knew what was going on. If Elly was so set against anybody knowing where she was, he would have to go by her wishes.

The girl crawled into the open. And suddenly she twitched the coat out of Jim's grasp, grabbing the flashlight.

"Hey! What do you think you're doing?" Jim tried to snatch the light back, but Elly had jumped out of his reach. Then he slipped on some mud and went down on one knee.

"I'm going to hunt Mer! I saw her go— over that way—" Elly waved the torch so the beam swept the edges of the overgrown bushes. "It was just before the rain hit so hard. She must be stuck somewhere waitin' for it to quit."

"You can't find any cat out in this dark!" Jim protested. "They can hide under things and—"

"I can find Mer," Elly repeated with the same stubbornness, " 'cause I know just where she is. I told you, Mer thinks and I can sort of hear her thinking right in my own head. She's bad worried about something right now; she's in trouble maybe. And I've got to find her! So I'll take the loan of this coat," Elly had already struggled into it, though the cuffs hung well over her hands and the hem dragged in the wet mud. But she used the belt to jerk it up, making extra folds above her waist.

How much of what Elly said was the truth? Jim, watching her, thought that at least Elly believed it all. Maybe the cat *was* caught someplace, crawled in to get away from the rain and now could not get out.

And where was Tiro? Jim, picturing the black cat in his mind as hiding under a bush or someone's porch waiting for the rain to cease, was suddenly struck by another fleeting picture—Tiro running along a street with other cats behind him. Were they chasing him? No, but there was something wrong, something Tiro feared. Rex—could Rex be loose and out hunting?

Jim tried hard to think of Tiro again, to see him, where he might be. But there was nothing, only a lingering impression of fear, of a need for haste.

He snapped free of that concentration in time to see Elly striding away, a dark shape outlined by the glimmer of the flashlight's beam she directed before her.

"Hey, where're you going?" Jim hurried after her. Even if the rain was now only a drizzle, he saw no reason to go out hunting a cat. Didn't everyone say cats were very good at looking after themselves? But were they, where there were dogs, and cars—and people who set traps to catch them and cart them off to be gassed or something the way some of the animal controls did? Tiro—somehow Jim was now as sure as Elly that Tiro and Mer were in danger. Though he had not the slightest idea of where to hunt.

The storm had not been a part of their plan. Tiro snarled silently as he bounded along, avoiding the larger pools before him. He hated the feel of wet fur.

Mer's signal. She had welcomed the first of the refugees aboard the shuttle. But it had taken them longer than he had counted on to work the cage latches. Then, of all the imprisoned ones, only a dozen had enough of the old blood to answer his signals. Three of the captives had been very quick and able in their response. They could not move as fast as they wanted to, for five of the cats carried kittens.

The instinct in Tiro's brain which would always lead him to home on the ship was fully awake. They had one more street to cross before they could take cover under the brush along the edge of the park where the shuttle had been hidden. He swerved toward the curb and those behind him padded in his wake. Car coming, Tiro crouched low. But the lights, gleaming through the rain, did not touch the small band gathered on the sidewalk.

Now!

They took the street at their fastest gait. But when they reached the bushes Tiro dropped back, sending his band on ahead. Mer was calling, her send-thought coming in steady and clear.

Two other shadows broke away from the general dark ahead to join the band. Those were not of the party Tiro had led, but they had caught the signal also and were drawn to it. He wondered how many of the kin would come. Some had become too much a part of this barbaric world. That part of their minds that should be awakened was withered away, bred out of them during the long centuries their generations had spent on this planet without teaching or exercise in the proper use of what had once been theirs. But the Ka'ats must do what they could to aid these long-lost brothers and sisters.

Tiro paused for a moment to give a quick lick across his wet fur. The sooner this night was over the better. Perhaps there would even be time to take a short nap in the garage bed before the humans began stirring in Jim's house.

Those humans. Tiro licked again. He believed they would be leaving soon, from what he had overheard and picked up from stray thoughts. Mostly Jim's thoughts, for sometimes the boy seemed almost as clear as if he could thought-send, as good as a young untrained cubling. Not that that mattered.

Tiro stopped licking. No, as he was a truthful Ka'at, he would have to admit it did matter. There was something about the boy— not that a Ka'at could be a friend to a human. But Jim was not like the usual human who was shown in tapes as a warning to scouts. He was not mind-bound, nor thoughtless of all but his own kind, not—

The Ka'at shook his head, the better to scatter such ideas out of his mind. It did not matter what Jim was, all that mattered was Tiro's own job. And he had better get to it. He slipped along under the wet branches, with such skill and ease that few of them dumped any water, and caught up quickly with the small group of cats bound for the ship.

"It ain't far now," Elly gave another impatient tug at the trailing skirt of the coat which *would* work out of the lump draped over the belt and try to trip her up. "Mer's there." The torch beam struck full against a black lump of bushes stuck all together. Jim thought that, since they had crossed two deserted streets, one still lighted, they must be coming close to the park. Perhaps those bushes marked the boundaries.

"Wait!" he caught at Elly's arm. Had he or had he not seen something moving over in those bushes? Under the pressure of his fingers on her wrist Elly's hand moved, holding the light. There was no wind now, so why had those branches shook a little as if something had just brushed under them?

"Mer's there."

"Did you see her?" Jim demanded.

"No. I just know it." Elly twisted free of Jim's hold to cross the third and last street. This was the edge of the park, and the park at night was dangerous. Jim tried to catch again at the big wrinkle of coat covering Elly's shoulders, but she dodged without even looking around. A moment later she was crouching. Holding the flashlight in one hand she used the other to sweep the branches away from the very same place Jim had seen the limbs moving. Lifting the tip of one they saw an opening like a tunnel running crookedly, so one could only see a pace ahead at a time.

The flashlight winked out.

"What happened?" Jim demanded. "Let me have it! Maybe if I shake it or something—"

"No!" Elly was as firm on that point as she had been stubborn earlier. "The light's all right. Only we can't use it, not here. We don't want them to know we're comin'—" She was already on her hands and knees crawling into that small, hidden path.

Did not want *who* to know they were coming, Jim asked himself, for he had a feeling Elly would not answer. Instead there came a kind of hiss from her, not unlike the hiss Tiro would give when he was annoyed.

"Be quiet. You make a lot of noise and maybe—" She did not finish the sentence and Jim realized, since he could no longer see her in the gloom, she was moving away along the passage.

There was nothing to do but drop to his hands and knees and, in a short time, to his stomach, and wriggle along a few inches at a time, feeling the way before him. His heart beat fast and his mouth felt all dry inside. He did not want to do this but if Elly could, then he was not going to leave her alone. What were they hunting along this very small and secret path?

Twice Jim ran into a bush, once painfully scratching his face because he did not make the proper turn. He had to go slowly, feeling with one hand for the open space which marked the trail, swinging that hand from right to left to keep the right direction.

Then he caught sight of a light to his right as the path made another of those sudden loops. It was not a street light, for it was of a pale, greenish shade. But the gleam held steady in one place, as if it were as fixed as a lamp. Between him and it hunched a dark bulk which he knew was Elly. He stopped as she hunkered down so he could look over her shoulder to what lay beyond.

There was a—a thing—a little larger than the garage. Jim could not be sure, for the light coming from a hole in its side did not show all of it. Into that hole cats were moving, each stopping to touch noses for an instant with a single one of their kind who stood on the outside of the opening.

Then the last cat disappeared, except for a very large black one.

"Tiro!"

The black cat whirled, his ears flattened, his eyes agleam in the pale light of the door. But Elly had torn her way out of the bush and was already running towards the other cat.

"Mer! Oh, Mer, I thought you was lost!"

7

Ka'at Justice

ELLY WAS ON her knees by the door from which the greenish light came. But Tiro, hissing, his tail lashing, stood between the girl and Mer.

Jim staggered, put his hands to his ears. Only he was not really hearing that snarling voice, not with his ears; it was ringing inside his head.

"Go away!"

Mer had moved forward towards Elly, paying no attention to Tiro. She slipped past him into Elly's arms, reaching up a paw to pat at the girl's chin.

"Tiro?" Jim hesitated. The black cat was

now staring at Mer rather than at the boy. There was a flash of brighter light within the doorway.

Elly set Mer down and went towards the door on hands and knees, the grey-white cat in the lead.

"Elly!" Jim called, "where are you going?"

She did not even turn her head to look at him. "With Mer."

Jim squatted down so that his eyes were closer to those of the black cat. "Tiro—what is happening?" He was shaken and afraid. Cats could not read his mind, or "talk" that way, they just couldn't!

"I am not a cat." There came a firm answer to that.

Jim blinked. "Then what are you?"

Tiro only stared back straight eyed. And Jim's uneasiness grew.

"You are too a cat," the boy said slowly. "But—you're something else. Maybe I—you —somehow you can talk to me—in my head. Tiro, what is happening? Please, tell me!" Jim begged. Fright shook his voice. "What is this thing—and what are all these cats doing here?"

Tiro's ears were still flattened to his skull; he looked fierce. And Elly was halfway through the door, crawling in after Mer who had already disappeared.

"You will tell," Tiro's word-message reached the boy. "Let you go now and you will have *them* know—"

"I don't know what you mean, Tiro, truly I don't!" Jim said. "Please make Elly come out. Then we'll go away and we won't tell anybody—"

"Come!" Tiro began to back toward the door, always facing Jim. And, without wanting to in the least, Jim found that he had to follow, just the same as if the black cat had a leash to pull him along.

He was shaking as he went down on hands and knees to crawl through the low door.

There was just one big room inside and cats were everywhere, wriggling under loops which bound them to the padded floor. Jim saw the banks of controls. This was a dream —it must be a dream!

"Here!" Tiro paused by one of those loops, but this one did not hold any cat. "Lie down!"

The boy saw Elly. She was across the

room, flat on the floor, pushing into a loop which Mer held up with her teeth to aid her. The girl's small face was lit with excitement.

"Get down," Tiro commanded. And to Jim his words in the mind hurt, as if they were meant to.

Jim stretched himself on the floor. Somehow, in spite of his shaking hands, he got the loop over his head and shoulders. The door had closed. He and Elly were shut in here with a lot of cats.

When he turned his head he saw Mer give Elly a quick lick on the cheek and then leap toward the front end of this room where she settled down before the control panel. Tiro watched Jim for a long moment and then stalked among the cats to join her.

Jim saw the black cat stare at the panel. There was an awful feeling as if the floor was going up at the same time Jim himself was going down. His insides twisted and he wanted to be sick. He closed his eyes. What was going to happen to them now?

"Jim?"

The boy opened his eyes. He felt strange all over, too light, his body pulling against the loop which was over him. This was still the same dream, he could not wake up. Where *were* they?

"Jim?" Somehow he moved his head without getting so sick that he had to vomit, but it was a close thing. He saw Tiro's head turn towards him, those green eyes watching him.

"There was no other way. We could not have left you when you had seen so much. But—" The mind words faded and Jim sensed Tiro's own uneasiness.

He and Elly had seen something they were not meant to see. But Mer, Mer had seemed to welcome Elly, and the girl had entered this place of her own will, not been compelled to come as Jim had been. So, perhaps Elly knew more—

"Elly?" the boy turned his head again. All the cats on the floor appeared to be asleep, but Elly, still huddled in Mrs. Dale's wet and mud-stained coat, was smiling, looking so happy that it changed her face a lot from the Elly he had known. Her eyes were closed, too. Maybe she was asleep like the cats.

"What's going to happen to us, Elly and me?" his voice sounded weak, as if he had been crying and did not want anyone to know.

"That will be decided."

"By whom—you and Mer?"

"No," Tiro turned his head away. His back faced Jim and somehow the boy knew he had been shut out.

In spite of his queasiness he felt sleepy, though he fought it. He had to know, to be ready. Instead his eyes closed firmly.

"You have broken all rules," Tiro did not look at Mer but his thought struck as hard as he could aim it.

"It was not of my doing entirely." Mer did not appear disturbed. "The girl child was far more receptive than any human I had been trained to handle. She traced me tonight. And did you not bring the boy? You spoke the truth when you said that they could not be allowed to go free after seeing the shuttle. Or was that the full truth, Tiro? They are children, would the closed-mind humans really have believed them?"

Tiro growled deep in his throat. "They would have brought searchers whether they were completely believed or not. Thus we would have lost the best landing site we had found. But what the Seniors will say—"

"Let us wait then until they do speak."

Tiro could not understand Mer. She had satisfaction in her thought. It was true that their rescue plan had been carried out successfully. But taking two humans might well cancel all the credit for that when they reached the headquarters ship. What had Mer to be satisfied about? She should be as uneasy as he was.

It was true that the girl had showed a far greater ability at thought-send than any human had shown in generations of tests. And the boy—Tiro had been able to communicate with Jim, even to the point of bringing him to the shuttle. Could it be that human and Ka'at could again communicate? But that could not be so. The time for any hope of re-establishing the ancient contact had long since passed.

Tiro thought about Jim. Oddly enough, though he had known other humans during his first scouting trip, he had never established any closeness with them. In fact he had thought that the records of such alliances came close to being fables, though Ka'ats did not usually use their imaginations in that direction. Jim was a lonely boy and he looked upon Tiro as a friend. He had worried about Tiro, had planned to take him on the flight to the country. Tiro had read a lot in Jim's mind that had never been put into real words. He rumbled now as he remembered this or that which he had picked out of Jim's thoughts. But nothing would excuse Tiro and Mer from a full blame from the Seniors for what they had done.

Jim tried to roll over, not yet quite awake. The fact that he could not move seemed part of a bad dream. Then he roused enough to look around. The cats around him were stirring, slipping out of the loops that had held their bodies and heading toward the door. He saw Elly sitting up, rolling the sleeves of the coat higher to free her hands.

There was no sign of either Tiro or Mer.

"Elly," Jim managed to say hoarsely, "do you know where we are?"

She laughed. This was an Elly he did not know, an Elly who did not seem to care what happened to her.

"This here is a kind of airplane," she answered promptly, "only it goes a lot higher than a regular plane does. And now we've come to another one. This one fits inside of it sort of. Maybe we're goin' to the moon! I don't care!'' Her braids waggled as she laughed again. ''Maybe the moon's a lot better than where I've always been—''

Jim swallowed. He had been fumbling with the loop that held him and now it suddenly loosened so he could pull out of it. Elly was crazy, she *had* to be crazy!

''You mean we're on a flying saucer or something like that?'' he demanded.

''Don't know nothing about flying saucers,'' the girl returned. ''But here we are, ain't we? Mer and Tiro, they brought us here —with all these cats. Seems like they went to our world just to get the cats. Mer says they're kin from 'way back, that Mer's people once lived for awhile down there with us. Then something bad happened and for a long time the kind like Mer and Tiro, they didn't get to our world again. The cats that was left behind, they changed. Some of them got so different that they could not answer the signal at all.''

''Who told you this—Mer?''

Elly nodded.

''And what's all this about a signal?''

For the first time Elly's happy look was gone. ''Something bad, real bad, is maybe

111

going to happen to our world. Mer and the rest, they're afraid. So they came to take their kin away to where it's safe.''

"Something bad—'' Jim repeated. War? Was there going to be another war, maybe an atomic one?

"If they know, why can't they stop it?''

Elly looked at him scornfully. "How? People, they are sure pig-headed. Think they'd listen to any animal—like a cat—say they was doin' wrong? People always think they know best.''

She was right, Jim had to agree, "knowing best'' for others seemed to be something he had heard of all his life. And he could just imagine what would happen if Tiro, say, walked into the White House to tell the President not to start a war. Even if the President believed him, then other people would say *he* was crazy, listening to a cat! And Tiro could not go round the whole world thinking at people.

"Mer says we two are different. We understand when they think at us. People haven't done that for a long time,'' Elly went on. "That was how I could find Mer.''

"Maybe, but what do we do now?'' Jim came right to the point. "They've got us here.

Tiro said they were afraid we might tell about this ship—or whatever it is—and he had to take us. But are they going to keep us?"

"I don't care. Nothin' back there that I want anyway," Elly declared. "I want to be with Mer an' maybe have adventures. Granny's gone. An' maybe there ain't any home place that I can get to. But I'll find a place, me and Mer will!"

"I want to know what they're going to do—" Jim was not nearly so confident.

"Humans!" Leader Ana was startled so that the fur along her spine stiffened and arose. "It is impossible for us to deal with humans now! You will control their memories at once and return—"

"I claim the girl!"

There was silence, yet a visible wave of lifted heads, stiffening spine fur, rippled out across the assembly. Ana and Fledyi stared stonily at Mer.

"By the right of the old Law, I claim the girl." She had said it again and she was not wilting under the fury in the Seniors' gaze. "That custom too, is to be found in our history."

"A human cannot be tamed," Fledyi stated flatly.

"The girl has established mind-send with me. She is very young. Even *our* cublings must be taught. If she can be so reached, then she can also be taught. Is that not the logic upon which we pride ourselves?"

"Do you realize what claiming means, younger sister? You, and you alone, shall be responsible for her. Her acts will be considered yours. If she proves not-kin to us in her ways then will you be not-kin either, and your own kind shall drive you forth," Ana thought solemnly. "It is a task beyond most Ka'ats. Think well, younger sister, before you promise this, for your promise, once given, will stand for life."

"That I know also. But she is mind-kin. I cannot now leave her to that which may be coming to the humans."

"And the boy?" It was Fledyi who asked that. He looked beyond Mer to Tiro. They were waiting.

Tiro flexed his claws. At that moment he felt very unlogical, almost human, when he glanced at Mer. It was her reckless thoughtlessness which had gotten them into this. He did not want to make such an agreement for Jim.

Yes, the boy had shown some promise. But to claim him before all the Ka'at kin, to take on such a heavy responsibility, that was another matter. It was only logical that he should agree instead to change Jim's memory, return him on their next visit to pick up refugees, put him entirely out of mind. That was the sensible thing to do. But—he could not. If he did not match Mer now, he could never be the Tiro he thought himself to be. Willingly, unwillingly, he must follow Mer's lead. And then he must strive to be mind-kin with Jim. He could only hope that Mer was right—that, like cublings, these human young could be taught.

"I claim the boy," he said, and accepted all that that meant. At once, somehow, Tiro felt deeply, illogically, happy.

Elly gave a laugh and Jim, who had been inspecting the controls, looked quickly around.

"They done it! Mer an' Tiro, they've said we can stay with them!"

"How do you know—" Jim began, and then the certainty of what she said seeped into his own mind. Tiro—Tiro wanted him, truly wanted him!

Jim sat down on the padded floor. Now that the decision was made, he was beginning to feel free like Elly said. There was no one back on earth he cared for much with Dad and Mom gone, and there could be all sorts of adventures ahead. He and Tiro, Elly and Mer —it was like being drawn into a circle of warmth. The future would be very different, but he was not afraid any more, not with the kin about him. Kin? One small part of his mind asked, and then that, too, was satisfied and accepted the rightness of what was here and now. Jim looked toward the door. Tiro would be coming soon. It was all right, everything would be everlastingly all right from now on.

ARCHWAY
PAPERBACKS

Other titles you will enjoy

29833 BASIL OF BAKER STREET, by Eve Titus. Illustrated by Paul Galdone. The Mystery of the Missing Twins was one of the strangest and most baffling cases in the famous career of Basil— Sherlock Holmes of the mouse world. ($1.25)

29733 DANNY DUNN, INVISIBLE BOY, by Jay Williams and Raymond Abrashkin. Illustrated by Paul Sagsoorian. Danny Dunn and his friends have fun experimenting with a new invention created by Professor Bullfinch: a machine that can make them invisible. ($1.25)

29803 THE MOUSE AND THE MOTORCYCLE, by Beverly Cleary. Illustrated by Louis Darling. Ralph, a young mouse, is off to high adventure when he gets the chance to ride a shiny, new toy motorcycle. ($1.25)

29807 SKATEBOARDS AND SKATEBOARDING: *The Complete Beginners Guide,* by LaVada Weir. Illustrated with cartoons and photographs. This basic guide shows you how to ride, do tricks safely, care for your equipment, and how to buy or even build your own skateboard. ($1.25)

29816 MOSHIE CAT, by Helen Griffiths. Illustrated by Shirley Hughes. The true story of a Majorcan kitten's adventures and misadventures as he searches for and finds a loving home. ($1.25)

29805 ABRACADABRA! *Creating Your Own Magic Show from Beginning to End,* written and illustrated by Barbara Seuling. Everything a beginner needs for a smash debut, from making a hat to planning a project. ($1.25)

29814 DANNY DUNN, SCIENTIFIC DETECTIVE, by Jay Williams and Raymond Abrashkin. Illustrated by Paul Sagsoorian. Danny sets to work with Bleeper, his robot bloodhound, to track down the thief who robbed the safe in Midston's biggest department store. ($1.25)

29730 THE CITY UNDER GROUND, by Suzanne Martel. Illustrated by Don Sibley. Centuries after a nuclear holocaust, a boy who lives in a surviving underground city dares to explore the outside world. (95¢)

29817 FOG MAGIC, by Julia L. Sauer. Illustrated by Lynd Ward. When Greta walks through the fog, she starts off on an adventure that takes her back to the past of one hundred years ago. ($1.25)

(If your bookseller does not have the titles you want, you may order them by sending the retail price, plus 35¢ for postage and handling, to: Mail Service Department, POCKET BOOKS, a Simon & Schuster Division of Gulf & Western Corporation, 1230 Avenue of the Americas, New York, N. Y. 10020. Please enclose check or money order—do not send cash.)